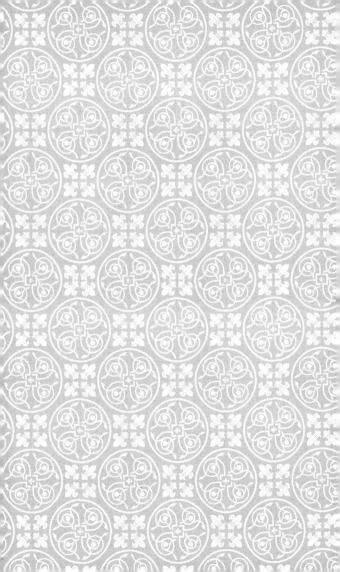

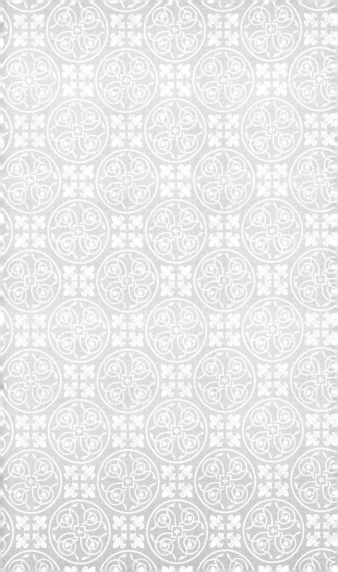

Rules for a Knight

Rules for a Knight

The Last Letter of
Sir Thomas Lemuel Hawke

ETHAN HAWKE

Illustrations by Ryan Hawke

ALFRED A. KNOPF
New York
2015

Ryan and Ethan Hawke are donating 100 percent of the royalties from this book to organizations working to help young people overcome learning disabilities.

THIS IS A BORZOI BOOK
PUBLISHED BY ALFRED A. KNOPF

Knopf, Borzoi Books, and the colophon are registered trademarks of Penguin Random House LLC.

Library of Congress Cataloging-in-Publication Data
Hawke, Ethan, [date]
  Rules for a knight : the last letter of Sir Thomas Lemuel Hawke / Ethan Hawke. — First edition.
    pages ; cm
  "This is a Borzoi book."
  ISBN 978-0-307-96233-1 (hardcover : acid-free paper).
  ISBN 978-0-307-96234-8 (eBook) 1. Knights and knighthood—Fiction. 2. Self-realization—Fiction. 3. Self-actualization (Psychology)—Fiction. I. Title.
  PS3558.A8165R85 2015   813'.54—dc23   2015020522

Cover design by Peter Mendelsund
Manufactured in United States of America
Published November 10, 2015
Reprinted One Time
Third Printing, December 2015

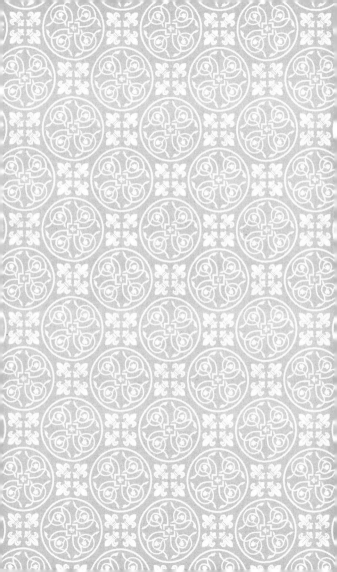

Rules for a Knight

Editor's Note

THIS letter was discovered in the early 1970s in the basement of our family farm near Waynesville, Ohio, following my great-grandmother's funeral. How it came to be there and its authenticity have been sources of much inconclusive debate. Our family does, however, lay claim to a direct lineage to the noble Hawkes of Cornwall, and Sir Thomas Lemuel Hawke was among the 323 killed at the Battle of Slaughter Bridge in the winter of 1483. The letter and rubric were originally written in Cornish and had been severely damaged at the time of their discovery. They were pieced together, adapted, and reconstructed by me, Ethan Hawke, from a literal translation provided by Dr. Linda Shaw of Missouri University at St. Louis. I tried to create a tone that was true to the integrity of the time, while making the letter accessible to my children. Please forgive any obvious errors. I assure you the mistakes are mine and not Sir Thomas's or Dr. Shaw's. When struggling to convey Sir Thomas's thinking, I have used expressions and turns of phrase found in the writings of other knights (named on page 171) to articulate what I could not. The illustrations were found with the text, reconstructed, and arranged here by my wife, Ryan Hawke. The Hawkes were originally Hawkers and worked with hawks, falcons, and other birds. We are a family with a long history of ornithology.

E.H.

Cornwall, 1483

My Dear Children, Mary-Rose, Lemuel, Cvenild, & Idamay,

A dark wind murmurs secrets into my ear as I write to you this evening. Perhaps this whisper is only the deceitful voice of fear, but I must admit, I am afraid I will never see you again.

This war with the Thane of Cawdor has raised in pitch, and so too has my belief that I will not live to enjoy the peace that follows. After my narrow escape at the Battle of St. Faegan's Fields, I began to feel compelled to pass on to you Grandfather's list of "Rules." His rubric will help instruct you should I be unable to do so in person. It's important that you, Mary-Rose, Cven, and Ida, realize these rules had been written for me, a young man on his journey towards knighthood, but they apply just as surely to an aspiring lady.

If I return safely home from tomorrow's battle, all the better; but should I not, then turn to these pages whenever you might look for my voice in guidance. I do not want you children to use my untimely death, or any setback that life may deliver, as an excuse not to take responsibility for yourselves.

Ida, on this day, the twenty-first of July, you are only four years old, and if my fears prove justified you will not remember any aspect of me. For this I am most sad, but none of you children yet know me as anything but the tall person who scolds or encourages you, or as a voice talking to your mother as you fall asleep. I have worked too hard in the last ten years and traveled too much, and now it seems I may miss your childhoods entirely. This comes as a blow. I have been looking forward to your growing up and hoped that we could, over time, know one another in a more meaningful way.

Tonight I will share with you some of the more valuable stories, events, and moments of my life so that somewhere deep in the recesses of your imagination these lessons might continue on and my experiences will live to serve a purpose for you.

When I was a young man I didn't know how to live. Evenings I would carouse with my friends, fighting, drinking, and wreaking havoc all through the night hours. My mother died when she gave birth to me, and all during my teenage years I'd leaned on that tragedy as an excuse for my own destructive behavior. Sometimes in a moment of reflection, I would seek solace in the chapel, my heart swollen with remorse over the suffering I had caused myself and others. My soul felt wild, and I could not discern for what reason I had been born. This lack of purpose weighed so heavily on me that at times I felt despondent, as if I were made of lead and sinking to the bottom of the ocean. Other times my idle nature made me feel so light and insignificant, I worried I might float away. Finally, this crisis inside me rose to a deafening drum. I decided to seek out the wisest man I could find and ask him to tell me how to live.

My mother's father, your great-grandfather, lived up on a wooded hill at the farthest reaches of our homeland, past Lanhydrock, up near Pelynt Barrow. Your great-grandfather had been one of the four surviving arrow retrievers for King Henry V's longbowmen at the Battle of Agincourt at the age of eleven. He was later knighted by King Henry himself. Widely admired throughout Cornwall, Grandfather was a powerfully built man with a wide gap between his front teeth. I had met him on only a handful of occasions, as he and my father had a troubled relationship. (Lemuel, you might remember Grandfather. He tried to give you a toy wooden dagger and you cried, "He looks like a dead person!" Grandfather laughed.)

I came to his door and knocked. When he answered I said boldly, "Everyone claims you are the wisest man of the realm. Please tell me how I should live. Why should I not cheat or steal? How do I keep from terrible attacks of fear? Why am I so inconsistent? Why do I do what I know I should not? Am I weak or am I strong? Am I kind or cruel? I have been all these things! I don't even truly understand the difference between right and wrong. Just and unjust. And what does any of it matter, since in no time at all everybody I know will be rotting in the ground feeding worms?"

The old man said, "Would you like some tea?"

"Yes," I responded, unsure if he had heard what I said.

"Then sit down for a moment."

Anxiously, I did as I was instructed.

My grandfather set down two blue cups and poured some tea into the first, but he did not stop when the cup was full. He kept pouring and pouring until the hot tea spilled all over the table and splattered onto the floor.

"What are you doing?" I shouted, jumping up, hot tea scalding my legs.

"You are like that cup spilling over," said my grandfather. "You cannot retain anything. There is too much going on and you are splashing everywhere, burning what you touch."

I stared at him.

"Look at this cup," he said, pointing to the other small blue ceramic cup still sitting on the white tablecloth. "It is not overanxious to be filled. It sits patient, unmoving, and empty." Carefully, he poured a small amount of tea into that cup. "You must be like this," he stated with a mischievous grin, gesturing to the steam gently rising from the second blue cup. "Answers to your questions will come, but if you are not still and empty, you will never be able to retain anything."

I sensed my shoulders drop and a smile come over my face.

"I knew I'd come to the right place," I congratulated myself.

"Hmmm," mumbled my grandfather.

There was a long stillness.

"I'm glad you've come, Thomas," he said, piercing me with his ancient blue eyes. "I've been hoping you'd show your face at my door for a long time, and I will happily accept you as my squire, if that's what you want. But the first thing you must understand is that you need not have gone anywhere. You are always in the right place at exactly the right time, and you always have been."

He paused and looked at me even more deeply. "Do you know why King Arthur's knights could not see the mountain peak of Sca Fell?"

I shook my head no.

"Because"—he smiled gently—"that's where they were standing."

I was seventeen when Grandfather took me on as his apprentice. That was old for a squire. I had much to learn about chivalry. The first thing I was given was a small handwritten list entitled "Rules for a Knight."

I

Solitude

CREATE time alone with yourself. When seeking the wisdom and clarity of your own mind, silence is a helpful tool. The voice of our spirit is gentle and cannot be heard when it has to compete with others. Just as it is impossible to see your reflection in troubled water, so too is it with the soul. In silence, we can sense eternity sleeping inside us.

One time, on a sweltering August night, Grandfather and I made camp down by the ocean. He said, "While I teach you about the ways of war, I want you to know that the real struggle is between the two wolves that live inside each of us."

"Two wolves?" I asked, seated on an old log near the fire. My eyes were transfixed by the flames twisting uncomfortably in the night air.

"One wolf is evil," he continued. "It is anger, envy, greed, arrogance, self-pity, guilt, resentment, inferiority, deceit, false pride." He paused, poking the embers of our fire with a long stick he'd been carving.

"The other is good. It is joy, love, hope, serenity, humility, loving-kindness, forgiveness, empathy, generosity, truth, compassion, faith."

I considered that for a minute, then tentatively asked, "Which wolf will win?"

Sparks danced towards the stars as the old man stared into the glare of the flames and replied: "Whichever one you feed."

II

Humility

NEVER announce that you are a knight, simply behave as one. You are better than no one, and no one is better than you.

Without the blacksmith, the knight's sword would splinter into shards. Without the carpenter, a lady's wagon would collapse. Without the mason, the castle would crumble. Without the seamstress, the King would ride to church naked as a fool. All living things rely on each other. If there were no earthworms, the soil would be depleted, grow no food, and we would die. Understanding that he relies on all that surrounds him, a knight is kind above all. He knows he will need many friends. Proper manners are not trivial. Being polite is part of our daily meditation on the equality of mankind. A knight says "please" and "thank you." He never charges into battle alone. His kindness, compassion, and humility serve as his banners that many may rally around.

For Grandfather, humility was the essential element to a magnificent life. Humility is the ability to see yourself in the context of a much larger world. The stars are magnificent. They are always there whether you see them or not. Aspire to be like the soil after the March rains, wet, open, and receptive.

"Be humble or get humbled," Grandfather would say. "A knight is never so arrogant as to think he has nothing left to learn." He loved talking to me while we would ride horseback on one of his various errands, almost teaching himself as he was teaching me.

"When people speak, listen." This was a point he would consistently stress. "As much as you like to be heard and understood, so does everyone else."

As the youngest child of a wealthy family, he had witnessed most of his brothers and sisters destroyed by a false sense of entitlement.

They expected the world to give them everything, and they all, in turn, were colossally disappointed when it did not. Instead of being grateful for the pony they received for Christmas, they would be disappointed they had not gotten a stallion.

"There is nothing so helpless as the child of a rich man," Grandfather liked to say. "The push and pull of the oceans, the sun rising and falling, the flow of the seasons, the waxing and waning of the moon, none of that is enough for them."

"But what about you?" I once asked. "You are the child of a rich man."

"Hmmmm," he grumbled. "Just give thanks I've lost most of my money. If you can lose it in a shipwreck, it isn't really yours!" He slapped his saddle and chuckled to himself. "Expect nothing, and you will enjoy everything!"

We were crossing the craggy rocks of the Hogwill Fells, twelve of us riding in formation. By late morning we came to an impasse where the road split into three paths. We could choose the high road, which appeared beautiful with a glorious view but treacherous and steep to climb; the low road, which descended and had an easy, muddy look to it; or a middle path, which was a combination, some parts up, some parts down. Grandfather led us along the center path. When unsure of my footing, I have always been served by remembering that choice.

My pony ambled close behind Grandfather's stallion, Triumph.

"What was the wisest thing you ever heard King Henry the Fifth say?" I asked. In those early days I couldn't stop asking questions.

"Modest success," he answered.

"What do you mean?"

"The last time I saw the great King, I was only sixteen and he said to me, 'I wish you modest success.'"

"I don't understand."

"Neither did I." Grandfather winked.

Continuing on that spring morning, we went up and down the meandering path until our horses grew thirsty. Abruptly, Grandfather stopped at the bank of the clear Hogwill River. He pointed down at some minnows.

"See how freely those fish swim and dart about? See how happy they are?"

He just watched the shivering silver minnows and chuckled to himself. In those early days of assisting him, I often wondered if he might just be a crazy old man. He was certainly eccentric.

"Since you are not a fish," I asked, gently prodding him, "how do you know what makes fish happy?"

The rest of the men behind us laughed, and I swelled with an impertinent pride.

"Since you are a squire and I am a knight"—Grandfather returned the volley—"how do you know that I do not know what makes fish happy?"

"Yes, that's true," I continued. "But since I am a lowly squire, and cannot possibly know what a distinguished knight like yourself must know . . . doesn't it follow that you, a knight, cannot know what a simple fish feels?"

The men chuckled their approval at my rising confidence.

"Wait a minute!" Grandfather said, dismounting Triumph and suddenly taking off his boots and socks. "Let's get back to the original question: you ask, how do I know what makes fish happy? From the terms of your question, you admit that I know what makes fish happy!"

I was momentarily flummoxed.

"You see," Grandfather went on, easing his old, tired feet into the cold water, "I know the joy of the fishes through my own joy. We swim in the same river."

III

Gratitude

THE only intelligent response to the on-going gift of life is gratitude. For all that has been, a knight says, *"Thank you."* For all that is to come, a knight says, *"Yes!"*

In the first year of my training, I had a terrible toothache. Grandfather and I spent a long autumn afternoon in a field constructing a fence for some horses. I groaned constantly about how difficult it was to dig a hole when my tooth hurt so badly. I complained every time I swung the sledge, hammering the posts into the stiff earth, that my mouth felt as if it would explode. I told Grandfather, "If only my tooth didn't throb so much, everything would be perfect and I could enjoy my labor."

Months passed. It was winter, and Grandfather and I were engaged in more carpentry. This time we were in the back barn repairing an old stall. I spent most of that morning cursing the bitter cold and complaining how I could barely feel my fingers. Then Grandfather asked, "But how is your tooth?"

"Oh, it's fine," I said.

"Well, then!" He grinned. "What a remarkable day this must be!"

The quiet of each morning, the tangible bond of friendship, a snowball fight, warm water on your skin, laughing until your stomach hurts, a job well done, a shooting star that you witness alone; the simple joys are the great ones. Pleasure is not complicated.

IV

Pride

NEVER pretend you are not a knight or attempt to diminish yourself because you deem it will make others more comfortable. We show others the most respect by offering the best of ourselves.

Arrogance is born of insecurity. Pride is different. It is born of dignity, self-worth, and self-respect. We all see the world through the prism of our identity. If our self-worth is low, it affects everything we do. The point of life is to contribute to others, but without a certain self-regard, it is sometimes difficult to make breakfast.

A knight takes pride in his handwriting. He keeps careful track of his saddle, his boots, and his weapons. He cleans and cares for his tools, animals, and his person. He carries his own bags. The laces of his boots are strapped tight. Always prompt, a knight is not casual with the time of others. There is no dirt in Heaven, and we are here to make the earth as much like

Heaven as we can. A knight is the best kind of servant, leaving every space he enters brighter and cleaner than when he arrived. His surroundings reflect his state of mind.

Constant awareness of even the smallest detail trains your mind to be observant and conscientious. A knight knows where he keeps his flint box; when he pulls it from his pocket, the cotton inside is dry. A knight does not need to be told how many arrows are left in his quiver. Responsibility, awareness, and self-knowledge are his allies. Forgetfulness is his enemy. His mind is not in the future. He is fully engaged in what he is *doing*.

I can still smell the pipe smoke from Grandfather's breath as both his arms wrapped around my body, his cheek touching my cheek, finally teaching me to shoot a bow and arrow.

"Be proud, not arrogant. Back straight, head high. Stand like you deserve to be here."

Shadowing himself to my body, he adjusted me ever so lightly. With our hands together we raised the bow. "Shoot for nothing. When an archer shoots for a prize, he gets tight." Still together like a hand in a glove, we notched the arrow.

I could feel Grandfather's body was neither at rest nor rigid. He was firm yet pliant. "When you shoot to impress, your eyes divide. You see two targets," he whispered. We drew back the bowstring. "Your skill has not changed, but the imagined prize separates you." Our eyes seeing as one, we focused the arrow on a dark knot in a sycamore tree thirty yards away. "Thinking more of the prize than of his target, a knight is drained of power by the need to win."

Slowly, without me even noticing, Grandfather removed himself from my body. I stood alone, arm back, arrow at the ready.

"Thinking of nothing, you can let go."

When you train hard, do your best, and strike the mark, pride comes all by itself.

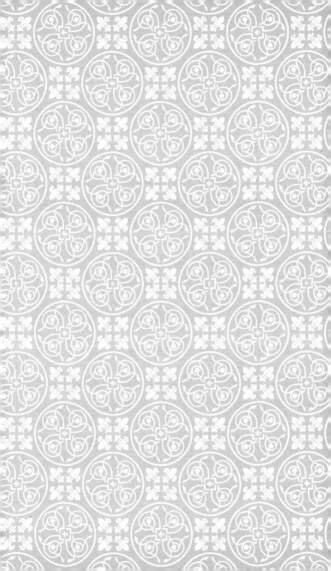

V

Cooperation

EACH one of us is walking our own road. We are born at specific times, in specific places, and our challenges are unique. As knights, understanding and respecting our distinctiveness is vital to our ability to harness our collective strength. The use of force may be necessary to protect in an emergency, but only justice, fairness, and cooperation can truly succeed in leading men. We must live and work together as brothers or perish together as fools.

efore long Grandfather took on another young squire. His name was Roan Sean Hamilton. He was Black Irish, fast, strong, intelligent, funny, and extremely handsome. He was an orphan. Grandfather often seemed more taken with him than with me. As skilled a swordsman as I was becoming, Roan was faster and stronger. As good a rider as I was, Roan was simply better. There was a young noblewoman, Cordelia, who lived down the road from us. I had long imagined that, when I reached a certain age, Cordelia and I would be wed. She fancied me too, of that I was certain, until Roan came to live with us. It was obvious immediately that she loved him.

I was in agony. At first I had liked Roan,

but the more time I spent with him the more I came to believe that he was humiliating me: his excellence mocked my mediocrity. Once, after some poor behavior on my part, which I cannot bring myself to confess to you children, Grandfather took me into the barn and slapped me hard across the face. "What is wrong with you?" he asked.

"He's better than I am at everything," I stated flatly.

"Is it not possible," Grandfather said with ferocious eyes, "that you both can be outstanding?"

A few weeks later Grandfather was called on an important assignment: to put down a rebellion led by the Duke of Easton and rescue the much-loved Philip Trelawny and his children, who were being held hostage. Grandfather didn't really want Roan or me along with him. We were still only twenty-one. Too eager for the thrill of battle, we refused to stay home.

The rescue of Trelawny was accomplished with a bold maneuver designed by Grandfather. However, at sunset of that evening on the edge of the Sedgemoor River, just south of Hell's Stone, brave young Roan was killed when an Easton arrow entered through the back of his neck and tore out the front.

It was clear what a waste of time my jealousy had been. I was still a deliberate, often plodding swordsman, my riding was improving at an even slower rate, and Cordelia was now in love with the son of our stable master. I missed Roan and realized only too late that his excellence did not humiliate me. He had challenged me and made me stronger. His death was a horrible way to learn such a lesson. The image of him unable to breathe, dying in the brilliant light of a Sedgemoor sunset, still haunts me.

I learned that evening that rain falls equally on all things. Jealousy, fear, and anger are obstacles to a knight's first goal: a clear mind. Through his practice a knight should cultivate an open, unclouded mind, so that his instincts will guide him and he is free to act spontaneously. Understanding that our "talents" are simply gifts we have received brings humility to our actions. It also allows us to appreciate the "talents" we see in others as expressions from the same universal source. There are only two possible outcomes whenever you compare yourself to another, vanity or bitterness, and both are without value.

In the confused and sorrowful haze after Roan's death, Grandfather and I were rushed to France as reinforcements for a decisive battle in Calais. In a few days, I was knighted. That, too, was disappointing to me. I had hopes of being knighted by the King, as Grandfather had been, but circumstances did not conspire to suit my fancies. I was knighted on the battlefield by the Bishop of Folkestone simply because, once defeated, the French knights would not surrender to ordinary soldiers and there were not enough English knights to take all the prisoners. Hence, at the age of twenty-one, I became a knight, but in the wake of Roan's death I felt little cause to celebrate.

Returning home, I continued to serve under Grandfather alongside the proud Knights of Lanhydrock. The men I've come to know are among the finest that I have ever encountered, and I am proud to call them friends. Many of them will ride with me tomorrow morning.

VI

Friendship

THE quality of your life will, to a large extent, be decided by with whom you elect to spend your time.

When I was first knighted, the Lanhydrock order totaled more than fifty in number. The following year, however, only seventeen of us survived the horrible six days that came to be known as the Battle of Lostwithiel. In the months following that short, hellish week, we went about the business of "victory," by burying the dead, nursing the wounded, putting out fires, rebuilding houses, and mending the damage in the neighboring farms.

One day, beside the tower of St. Brevita, a crowd had gathered around a child, eight or nine years of age, who was deathly ill, practically blind with a fever and sobbing endlessly. This is where I first came to know Sir Richard Hughes, a new knight of my order with a round belly and rich brown eyes. He was called upon to try to heal the small child. A skeptic in the crowd, who was still loyal to the Earl of Warwick, watched as Sir Richard laid hands on the young boy and whispered peaceful, calming words of prayer into his ear. The skeptic shouted out, mocking the knight for believing that his ancient whispers and primitive style of healing could have any power. In front of all the townspeople, Sir Richard answered, "You are an ignorant fool." The skeptic's derision became angry. His face reddened, and his hands began to shake with humiliation and rage. Before the skeptic could gather himself to shout back or raise his fist in violence, Sir Richard spoke again. "When a few words have the power to make you so angry, why would others not have the power to heal?"

As you all know, Sir Richard was to become my best friend. He was adroit at many things. Easy with both men and women, he enjoyed the social elite and the salt of the earth equally.

He had a small potbelly, short chubby arms, and the appearance of a friendly brown bear.

Remember, a friend does not need you to impress him. A friend loves you because you are true to yourself, not because you agree with him. Beware of grand gestures; the real mettle of friendship is forged in life's daily workings.

Always a source of calm, a knight or a lady is a reliable companion in times of turmoil. Perhaps more significantly, though, a good friend is also one to whom others rush to tell their good news. It's difficult to explain, but in some ways it can be easy to be supportive when your friend is hurt or sad. You may find it is more challenging to be wholeheartedly supportive when extreme good fortune befalls a friend and not you.

In the days after the Earl of Warwick was defeated, I was awarded a medal of honor from the King. Sir Richard was the first to hoist me on his shoulders. He was laughing, and his red face beamed with genuine delight.

VII

Forgiveness

THOSE who cannot easily forgive will not collect many friends. Look for the best in others and yourself.

very great knight has weaknesses. You will be no different. Where there are peaks, there will be valleys. You can be angry with yourself when you have disappointed, but let those feelings pass over and through you. Like a dead branch falling from a tree, which then decomposes and nourishes the soil, your disappointments can transform into the elements of change and growth. You will make mistakes, and people you love will make mistakes. But remember to judge yourself not at your worst but at your best. A knight knows that "success" is most easily measured by how he handles his disappointments.

We do not need a "perfect" family or the "ideal" community. The one we have is good enough with which to begin our work. To head north, a knight may use the North Star to guide him, but he will not arrive at the North Star. A knight's duty is only to proceed in that direction.

Shortly after you were born, Lemuel, your mother and I were walking through Saltash on our way home from a visit with your aunt Lizbeth. We came upon a young lord, no more than nine or ten, in a tyrannical rage, berating his servants for stopping his carriage over a large muddy puddle. I remember feeling embarrassed by the young lord's arrogance and passing him by. Your mother stopped, handed you to me, walked through the murky water, and carried the young lord to dry ground. Immediately he chided his servants, saying, "You are useless!" and ran inside, offering not even a glance of thanks to your mother. We continued walking on towards home. After a long time of glowering and grumbling to myself, I said, "I don't know why you helped that brat!"

Your mother turned to me and said, "I set that boy down hours ago, but I see you are still carrying him."

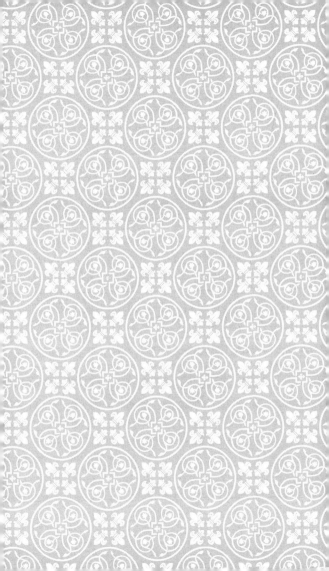

VIII

Honesty

A DISHONEST tongue and a dishonest mind waste time, and therefore waste our lives. We are here to grow, and the truth is the water, the light, and the soil from which we rise. The armor of falsehood is subtly wrought out of the darkness and hides us not only from others but from our own soul.

At a wedding celebration that Sir Richard and I attended as young men, there was an archery competition, and one particular young man from Wales had a friend who collected the arrows from the targets. Well, this "friend" kept reporting the Welshman's arrows closer to the center than they had actually landed. Sir Richard and I were exasperated when, at the festivities' end, these two hooligans sat at the wedding table with their prize, laughing as everyone congratulated this Welsh cheater on his fine marksmanship in winning the top honor. Richard and I were newly struck by the unfairness of the universe. Why were cheaters not always punished? Why did blessings come to terrible people?

"You don't need to stay up all night convincing people the sun will come up," Grandfather told us both when we complained to him. I didn't know what he meant. I had wanted that archery prize, for while I am by no means a great swordsman, I have always taken pride in my archery and it hurt to lose to a cheater.

There was no logic in my coveting that prize. My skills as an archer had proved reward enough, many times over. I can't even remember what the prize was. A turkey? A gold coin? Fifteen years later I learned that the Welshman was hanged by his own people. No one told me the exact cause, but I could divine the reason on my own.

That cheating Welshman is an obvious example of what not to do, but more often and more insidiously people lie because they feel the truth will cause pain to themselves or others. Don't fear suffering. The strongest steel is forged in the hottest fire. The facts are always friendly. Without a little agony, none of us would bother to learn a thing. The earth has to be tilled before the seeds can be planted. In much the same way, sometimes we have to be stirred and ripped apart so that the seeds of compassion, wisdom, and understanding can be firmly planted in us.

A knight does not protect the truth; he lives inside it and the truth protects him.

IX

Courage

ANYTHING that gives light must endure burning.

Courage is our ability and willingness to overcome our fear. Fear is nothing to be ashamed of, it is a powerful resource, reminding us to be wary, alert, and mindful. Fear is the dark and courage is the light. Fear is the call and courage is the answer. When struggling to find his courage, a knight relies on his breath. Sword fighting, archery, horsemanship—virtually every task I can think of is aided by an awareness of breath. It is the connective tissue of the universe, binding all living creatures together. By focusing on our breath, we are able to more adeptly inhabit our bodies and function on instinct. A wolf can ascertain all he needs to know about a man without ever exchanging words. So can you. Much of what is essential is intuitive. Pay attention: what you need to know is usually in front of you. There are no secrets, just things people choose not to notice.

When considering courage, it is impossible for me not to think of Sir Richard. The most dangerous mission Grandfather ever gave us was when we were left to guard the bridge at Barrow. There was a band of about twenty thieves that were marauding across the south of Cornwall. Grandfather anticipated them coming into our village from the north. To be safe, he positioned Sir Richard and me at an outpost by the Barrow Bridge, to leave the southern route protected. We built a large pyre to be lit in the event of an attack. The fire would be a signal that an attack had begun and that we needed aid. The unlit pyre was built on a high peak about a quarter mile from the bridge. Sir Richard and I camped up there. If we saw the marauders, we were to light the fire, run down to the bridge, and fight to prevent a crossing until our brothers joined us. Sir Richard became thoroughly consumed by anxiety that this plan was deficient. If we saw them too late, the thieves and killers could conceivably race to the bridge before us. "What if we could light the fire with an arrow? And be closer to the bridge? If we could light the pyre from the bottom of the mountain, we could always get to the bridge before our enemies."

He ruminated over it night and day. We practiced running down the mountain, but it was difficult terrain, and easy to fall if one hurried. This worried Sir Richard a great deal. He hated leaving success to chance. So we trained running down the mountain and Sir Richard practiced the shot. He built a new longbow and worked with it over and over. There was a rock from which he could get sure footing and launch the arrow accurately. Often he would make the shot. But just as often he would miss. He practiced more.

"Why are you so nervous? They probably won't come south," I said.

"It's the word 'probably' I don't like," he replied.

He couldn't sleep. I tried to relax him by playing cards. He was too nervous. So we would practice making the run from the rock to the bridge five times a day, ten times a day, then twenty times a day. I was in the best physical condition of my life. But still, I thought, they won't come from the south.

But come they did, and to our surprise with near forty filthy dogs running beside them. These men had no flag.

Sir Richard and I tore down the mountain. I was to run ahead to guard the bridge. He was to light the pyre. Sir Richard leapt to his rock, and with the longbow—his body acting on habit—he lit the arrow, just as he had practiced, and went to launch it. What he didn't anticipate were the dogs. They charged Sir Richard like wolves at a rabbit, but still he did not hesitate. His arrow soared, hit its mark, and quickly set the pyre ablaze. The smoke could be seen for fifty miles. Sir Richard tried to scamper to his position on the bridge with more than ten dogs biting and ravaging his body. I shot several of the mangy hounds with my bow. But there was little I could do; most were too close to him. I had to leave my position. The fight was the worst I have ever known. These men were brutal and their animals rabid with terror. It was only an hour before our brothers were behind us, but it was a gruesome hour. When it was over, half of Richard's left arm had been mangled and he had a small hatchet stuck in his back. Strong as an ox, he miraculously lived.

Back at his home, I visited him often during his recovery.

"How did you make that shot?" I asked. "When I saw those dogs charging at you . . . I have to admit I nearly lost hope. You had been so nervous every time we merely walked through it! How in God's name did you keep your poise?"

"That's why we practiced so much," he said with a laugh. "And you wanted to play cards!

"Truth is, Thomas"—he leaned in to me— "I did it for you. I realized that if I didn't make that shot . . . you were as good as dead. And . . . I like you!"

Later he told me when he was younger he learned the secret to performing under pressure: don't do it for yourself. Do it for someone else.

"I know your grandfather always tells us to think of nothing. But when I get scared I just think of someone I love."

As I tell this story I remember, Mary-Rose, that you already know this lesson of courage. Remember how apprehensive you were about speaking at Sir Richard's wedding to Alexandra? You tossed and turned in your sleep. All you had to do was throw some rose petals, walk the aisle, and recite a short poem, but the fear of failure had you tied up in knots. You admired Alexandra so much and didn't want to let her down. You practiced that poem over and over. Your mother taught you to breathe with the words, remember that? It was very much the same way Grandfather taught Sir Richard and me to breathe while letting loose an arrow. How beautifully you read that poem. Alexandra was so proud. And I know you did it for her.

> True love is a sacred flame that burns eternally,
> And none can dim its special glow or change its
>   destiny,
> True love speaks in tender tones and hears with
>   gentle ear.
> True love gives with open heart and true love
>   conquers fear.
> True love makes no harsh demands. It neither
>   rules nor binds.
> And true love holds with gentle hands the
>   hearts that it entwines.

Remember?

X

Grace

GRACE is the ability to accept change. Be open and supple; the brittle break.

Imagine that as a caterpillar transforms its shape, it must experience excruciating pain, while having no inkling of the exultation of flight.

Habit, routine, and too much consistency numb our minds and pave the road for us to sleepwalk through our lives. Nothing stays the same. Everything passes, and everything changes.

However, do not move too much. As an apple tree cannot bear fruit if it is too often transplanted, neither will a knight who is always building a new castle.

This may seem like contradictory counsel: to both accept the inevitability of change and attempt to remain constant. But to live well, sometimes you will need to hold two seemingly opposing truths, one in each hand, and carry them both comfortably. Nature creates its balance with opposites. We need the sun and the rain, the glacier and the desert. Likewise, inside ourselves, we must accept the inevitability of change while deepening and strengthening our foundation.

I would like to confess to you girls one of my clandestine prayers: that your legs be a little chubby or your nose just a touch crooked, because nothing gives a young woman permission to be weak-minded, lazy, and dull as much as being considered beautiful. Young people, women and men, often use the possession of beauty or wealth as permission to be uninteresting, undisciplined, and ill-informed. If they are fortunate enough to reach the age of twenty-eight or so, they become like coddled coyotes. Cute when little, but, upon adulthood, nasty, fearful, and living off the scraps of others.

Engaging in athletics is excellent for building self-confidence and cooperation. This is true for boys, but even more significant for young women, because it is so often absent from their lives. The world will not encourage you in this regard.

A lady—and this is true for gentlemen too, Lemuel—does not overconcern herself with her own appearance or with the appearance of others. She is not slovenly, far from it. She is meticulous in the care and cleanliness of her body. Her garments are an expression of her humility: clean, simple, well made, and flattering. With her words a lady is truthful. In her dealings she is authentic. A lady does not care for such false diamonds as knowing royalty. She knows herself and concerns herself with her own development, her ideals, and how they manifest in her actions. Is the cardinal more lovely than the rosefinch because its feathers are a deeper shade of red?

As you grow into maturity, do not concern yourself with aging. A rose is striking in full bloom only because it will never be so again, but a budding rose is also stunning, as are the dark petals of autumn. It is the fact that time is passing that creates its preciousness. A preoccupation with aesthetic beauty can be a distraction that leads young people away from pursuing a sincere exploration of their inner lives.

All of us are asked to surrender the superficial beauty of youth and step towards something greater. We are being made ready for the spirit world. Each wrinkle is a crack in the shell of our conceit. Our conceit must be pulverized for the soul to fly.

Sir Richard and I were riding one afternoon over the farmland along the edges of the Bodmir Moor. He paused on the road as a family traveled towards us. Their wagon was loaded, heavy with goods, furniture, and three young children. In those years, with the tremendous amount of political upheaval in England, this was a common sight.

"Excuse me, sirs," mumbled the mother, with a face twisted and unhappy. "We are traveling and looking for a new home. What are the people like in the town up ahead?"

"What are they like in the town where you came from?" Sir Richard asked in return.

"Oh, it was awful. People lied and cheated. We were terribly unhappy," the mother snarled, full of anger and disappointment.

"Oh, yes," the father added spitefully. "No one was kind. It was a dreary place, and we were glad to leave it."

"Well, there are many people like that in this town," stated Sir Richard. "I worry you will be miserable here too."

"Thank you very much," the father called out, shooting a scowl towards his wife. "Good riddance! We'll keep moving on."

The small children looked weary as the wagon rolled on.

Later, closer to evening, another family was seen traveling along the road. They were similarly loaded down with belongings and children.

"Excuse me," the father called out to us. "We are traveling and looking for a new home. What are the people like in the town up ahead?"

"What was it like where you came from?" Sir Richard asked, in a fashion similar to when he'd asked the previous family.

"Oh! We were so happy," the father replied. "The people were all kind and warm."

"We hated to leave," the mother added. "We had so many friends!"

"Well, don't worry, up ahead there are many people just like your friends." Richard laughed in his giant, warm way. "I think you will be very happy here."

XI

Patience

THERE is no such thing as a once-in-a-lifetime opportunity. A hurried mind is an addled mind; it cannot see clearly or hear precisely; it sees what it wants to see, or hears what it is afraid to hear, and misses much. A knight makes time his ally. There is a moment for action, and with a clear mind that moment is obvious.

Sir Richard had a celebrated white stallion that ran away. Friends and neighbors expressed their condolences: "How unfortunate! You must be so sad."

He said simply, "We shall see."

A week later the stallion returned, bringing with it two equally stunning mares. Sir Richard's friends and neighbors said, "Oh my, you are so lucky!"

Again Sir Richard answered simply, "We shall see."

A month went by, and Richard's eldest son, Jonathan, was thrown from one of the new horses and broke his leg. Jonathan cried in part from the pain but more because now he would not be able to ride with his fellow soldiers in the cavalry.

"How terrible for your boy!" lamented everyone, consoling Sir Richard. "What horrendous luck! I feel so sorry for your poor son. He must be terribly disappointed."

Once again Sir Richard answered, "We shall see."

In the following month the young men of Jonathan's cavalry unit were ambushed and killed in northern France. Neighbors came to my friend, saying, "Your son is the only one of our boys to survive! Aren't you the lucky one!"

"We shall see," he answered.

Remember, it is possible that it is not the sun that goes down; perhaps it is the earth that turns. No one is really sure, but one fact is clear: things are not always as they seem.

XII

Justice

THERE is only one thing for which a knight has no patience: injustice. Every true knight fights for human dignity at all times.

In the small fishing village by the Warlegan River, a woman was washing clothes when she saw a helpless calf floating downstream. She threw down her work and jumped in the water to save the animal. Happily, the calf was recovered.

The next day, two more calves were seen floating down the river. One was saved, the other lost. By the end of the week, several cows, many sheep, and a few horses had been rescued. Many more animals had floated by, already dead. The townspeople were confused and scared. They set watches day and night by the river's edge to try to rescue the live animals. A few people had even claimed to see a dead child disappearing downstream, trapped underneath some burnt branches. Believing they were doing the best they could, the townspeople worked hard, kept watch, held vigils, lit candles, and prayed in a state of nervous apprehension, but dead livestock and freshly burnt wood kept floating down the Warleggan.

It was at that point that Grandfather, Richard, myself, and a few other knights of our order rode by and were told what was happening. Grandfather was the first person to ask the obvious question, "Has no one gone upstream?"

A knight sets out to illuminate the darkness in society, not from its leaves but from its roots. This is how justice will be realized. Find the source.

XIII

Generosity

YOU were born owning nothing and with nothing you will pass out of this life. Be frugal and you can be generous.

There have always been two ways to be rich: by accumulating vast sums or by needing very little.

Possessions can be, and most often are, a distraction from the real work of a knight's life. A lion doesn't own anything at all, yet we all know his power. If a knight has amassed personal wealth, he does not weigh his spirit down with trunks of gold. Give freely and easily to all allies in the struggle for a just world where no child goes uneducated or unfed, where the health of everyone is responsibly cared for, and where ideas are openly and richly expressed. Give aid to all who are working towards vigorous stewardship of our land, waters, and animals. Do not waste money on extravagances. A knight knows there are too many who are suffering to take pleasure in being frivolous. If a knight finds himself without a full purse, he does not overly concern himself with this either. The quality of a lady's character determines her worth, not the coins in her purse, or the price of her garments.

The peregrine falcon is the swiftest, most adept animal I have ever seen. It is worth noting that, like many birds, the falcon's bones are hollow. Travel light.

Once, Sir Richard and I were sent up to the far north of Scotland to help in a time of famine. A camp set up by missionaries was to house hundreds of displaced people who had lost their homes due to a storm of drought, war, and disease. Here I became aware of poverty on a scale that I had not previously known. Families were living in utter squalor. The smell of death was potent. Mud, filth, vermin, and despair seemed to be multiplying in the wells, and in the dry riverbeds. No fathers were to be found. One starving child looked up at Richard and me as we passed above him high on our horses. Richard handed the boy some sweet bread Alexandra had made us. Instead of devouring the cake as we imagined he would, the boy held it carefully in his hands, sprinted to his two younger siblings, and divided the bread into three pieces. Never had I witnessed such profound and simple generosity. I no longer felt pity for this starving young boy. I admired him. My character had never been tested like his, and if it ever was, I hoped I would respond with his integrity.

Many of the King's knights orient the work of their orders around the accumulation of wealth. Many great knights have indeed been extremely affluent. But I don't know of one fabulously rich knight who collects his own taxes.

Your grandfather was unusual in his position on the dangers attached to wealth. He loathed tax collecting but refused to turn a blind eye to those from whose pockets his money came. He always did the messy work of his life with his own hands. Whenever doubt would arise over the accuracy of our scale, Grandfather would allow each farmer to oversee the weighing of his crops. Many times I used to go with him from home to home to visit the families who lived on our land. He knew each child's name, and was aware of the details of every family's life. I remember once as we were touring our district, Grandfather made me note how much laughter we heard.

He said, "A hearty laugh is the telltale sign of good health."

That Christmas he and I attended a banquet hosted by the wealthiest knight of London, the Duke of Dorchester.

"Did you hear it?" Grandfather asked me as we left the duke's cavernous halls.

"Hear what?" I answered.

"There was no ingenuous laughter," he said under his breath. "There were cruel cackles and snide sniggers . . . Sometimes I think that the more wealth people accumulate, the less they laugh"—he leaned in close, whispering—"and the more they fear death."

He took a pause, considering what he had said. "I've begun to be dubious of any invitation that requires me to buy new clothes."

Around this time, due to his accomplishments in battle and immense popularity, Grandfather was asked to be Bishop of Cornwall. Everyone perceived this as a lucrative promotion that would confer prestige, honor, and wealth. But Grandfather thought it was absurd that religious positions were offered to men without a background in the ministry and managed to quietly pass on the opportunity.

"I am happy where I am," he confided to me. "I have friends. I'm good at what I do. And that is enough."

Then he added, "Besides, I've never known a funny bishop."

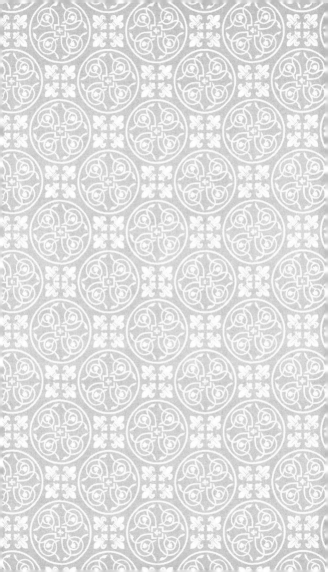

XIV

Discipline

In the field of battle, as in all things, you will perform as you practice; so practice hard. With practice, you build the road to accomplish your goals. Excellence lives in attention to detail. Give your all, all the time. Don't save anything for the walk home. The better a knight prepares, the less willing he will be to surrender.

Your sword should be sharp, balanced, and neither too heavy nor too light. Your foot should slide easily into your stirrup. Be the first to arrive and the last to leave. Oddly, with discipline, structure, and order, you will find there is freedom. Inside this kind of freedom, anything is possible. Without it, locating your saddle may take all morning.

Often we imagine that we will work hard until we arrive at some distant goal, and then we will be happy. This is a delusion. Happiness is the result of a life lived with purpose. Happiness is not an objective. It is the movement of life itself, a process, and an activity. It arises from curiosity and discovery. Seek pleasure and you will quickly discover the shortest path to suffering. Other people, friends, brothers, sisters, neighbors, spouses, even your mother and I are not responsible for your happiness. Your life is your responsibility, and you always have the choice to do your best. Doing your best will bring happiness. Do not be overconcerned with avoiding pain or seeking pleasure. If you are concentrating on the results of your actions, you are not dedicated to your task.

Grandfather did not live ten or twenty years ago. He lived in the present, just as you do now. "Be enthusiastic or be gone!" he would shout. "Be gentle and you can be bold."

You are not fragile. Engage. Being timid is often the result of being too self-critical and too self-concerned. A knight does not stop at each victory; he pushes on to risk a more significant failure. Grandfather used to say, "There are only two things worth hating: an easy life and too much success." Beware of needing or wanting too much praise. Believe in yourself. Discipline, preparation, and experience are the only tools you need.

A good example of Grandfather's mental discipline is his handling of the whole unfortunate situation that arose with our uncle, Sir Raulfe Trumpington.

Uncle Raulfe was actually Grandfather's first cousin. For some reason, everyone always called him Uncle. He was extremely affluent and known for his generous gifts. Once, he gave every Knight of Lanhydrock a gold brooch. It was expertly crafted and in the shape of a roaring lion. Grandfather insisted we all politely refuse the gift. "There is no such thing as a free brooch," he said cryptically.

He wanted us to simply tell Uncle Raulfe that, although we were immensely grateful, we were too concerned with the impoverished of our district to parade this kind of extravagant jewelry. Most all our knights thought Grandfather was being old-fashioned and ridiculous; some even accused him of being jealous.

Many of our men (I think all but Grandfather and myself) accepted the gift. A year later for Christmas, we were each delivered a Spanish stallion. Again, against Grandfather's wishes, many of our men accepted these beautiful horses.

"It's important," Grandfather told me as he bade me return the stallions to the Trumpington estate. From then on the gifts continued to everyone but us. Uncle Raulfe's generosity was seemingly endless.

A few years later I understood why. Sir Raulfe Trumpington was planning a large-scale conflict with a family on the outer reaches of Cornwall, along the Devon border. When the fight reached its crisis point, Uncle Raulfe called for the Knights of Lanhydrock to ride by his side. Many did. Grandfather and I stood still. We could see the whole affair as the arrogant waste of lives that it was.

That is where I lost Sir Richard. Manipulated by a false sense of loyalty to the Trumpingtons, Sir Richard ran into the hilt of a broadsword. I loved him. I have never let any of our knights wear those hideous gold brooches ever again.

Be resolute in your beliefs, my children. Your friendship cannot be bought.

Be cautious when anyone, even family, has too extreme an expectation from your behavior. Under the guise of love or loyalty, people can use guilt or fear to manipulate. A healthy conscience should be used like an internal compass: it is yours, not an instrument for others to play. Friends and family may at times ask you to be weak, they may even beg you, but all anyone *really* wants is for you to be strong.

XV

Dedication

ORDINARY effort, ordinary result. Take steps each day to better follow these rules. Luck is the residue of design. Be steadfast. The anvil outlasts the hammer.

everyone wants to be a knight; wanting is no great accomplishment. How hard you work is the difference between good and great, promising and masterful, squire and knight. To attain great wisdom, a knight knows he must live a long time. He remembers that his body is not his; it is a gift from his ancestors. Therefore, he does not poison his roots with intoxicants. He eats to live, and does not live to eat. He keeps his teeth and hands clean. His body and mind are kept sharp with daily exercise and contemplation. A knight steadies his nerves by getting enough sleep, but not too much. When his family and friends need him, a knight is at the ready.

Remember, Noah had to build the ark before the flood; likewise, you must not wait for the inevitable storms of life before you ready your mind. Thought precedes action. How we handle times of peace and calm will determine our behavior in moments of crisis.

I often think of the great siege of the ancient city of Caal. The invading soldiers positioned themselves in vast numbers outside the stone perimeter for six weeks. They tried to starve the people before charging in to attack and plunder what they hoped would, by then, be a depleted, malnourished military force. Instead, when the assault began, the attackers found the streets and homes empty of people and treasure. In previous years, the Knights of Caal had built underground tunnels reaching far into the outlying forests. So when the barbarous invaders surrounded the city, the entire population of Caal quietly, safely, and methodically escaped with all their children and possessions. Prepare.

XVI

Speech

Do not speak ill of others. A knight does not spread news that he does not know to be certain, or condemn things that he does not understand.

Gossip and an idle tongue are the enemies of friendship. Be careful too with exaggeration. A knight does not say that he *loves* his new scabbard, or that he *hates* himself. He knows words have meaning and does not misuse them. Disparaging yourself in order to rouse compassion in others is not humility. A lady remembers to breathe as she speaks. The words of her mouth and the meditations of her heart carry a lady's actions, just as her horse carries her body.

A knight does not whine. He concerns himself with affecting change, not burdening the world with his grievances.

Grandfather and I once rode through the high hills near the southern coast of Cornwall towards Zennor Castle. We had traveled far and were tired. The castle gates are set high atop rocky cliffs. As we climbed the steep slope, the sun began to set over the brooding landscape. I remember announcing, "Oh my, look at the sun! It is unspeakably ravishing!" Grandfather nodded in agreement. We continued on, and the higher we went the more splendid was the sunset. I continued my praise. "Grandfather, see how the sun is simply radiant! Look at the reds, and the streaks of burnt yellow! Isn't it wonderful?" Grandfather simply nodded, hunched over his horse. When we arrived at the gates, the sun had gone down and it was full night. I asked Grandfather, "Didn't you think the sunset was glorious? Why didn't you say anything?"

"The sun was speaking for itself," the old knight replied.

Later, as we were falling asleep, each comfortable in his own small cot high in the castle turret, I couldn't let it rest.

"Grandfather?" I whispered. "What could possibly be wrong with observing, taking note, and commenting on how beautiful the world is?"

There was a long silence, and I wondered if the old man had fallen asleep. Suddenly his voice, clear as the moonlight, spoke: "When we go fishing, what is the purpose of the bait?"

"To catch the fish," I answered.

"And what is the point of a rabbit snare?"

"To catch rabbits?"

"Of course," he answered. "And where is the bait when the fish is caught? Where is the snare when we have the rabbit?"

I was not sure of the correct answer, but tried simply "Forgotten?"

"Exactly. And the purpose of words is to convey ideas, right? Where are the words when the idea is grasped?"

"Forgotten?" I asked.

"Exactly," he said. "Now, where can we find a man who has forgotten words? That is a man I should speak with . . ."

He chuckled, and soon I heard his breath grow heavy with sleep.

I lay there unable to rest, looking out the small window above his bed. The moon was bright and full. This little window was nothing but a hole in the wall, yet it filled the whole room with light.

XVII

Faith

SOMETIMES to understand more, you need to know less.

As your father, I was present at each of your births, and I can attest there is the stuff of magic in each of you. Whatever well our lives are drawn from, it is deep, wild, mysterious, and unknowable. I am not in control of it, and neither are you. In fact, we are in control of very little outside of how we choose to handle each situation that presents itself. Don't forget there are some things that are so beautiful, so exquisite, that they should not be talked about, they can only be experienced.

Discovering, touching, feeling that which cannot be talked about is the splendid mission of every knight and lady. We find what we seek in this world, so be careful for what you wish.

Never make a big decision without first walking a mile. When in doubt, the Golden Rule is always there for you: do unto others as you would have them do unto you.

Trust the people whom you respect, whom you love, and who love you, but in matters of great importance, trust your own gut. Don't be fooled, and don't be hurried. There is plenty of time to make mistakes.

Why am I alive? Where was I before I was born? What will happen to me when I die? Why should I follow these rules? Ask the tough questions. Read how your elders have answered these same questions. Our ancestors were not fools.

You did not create the mountains, the oceans, the sun, or the rain. You did not even create yourself. So you can loosen your shoulders; the responsibility of the world does not rest on your back alone.

Beware of becoming too zealous about anything. People are often talking about a man so holy he can walk on hot coals, or a woman whose prayers are so divinely powerful she can dance on water. For me, walking on the earth has been miracle enough.

I remember a beautiful woman in our village, Liza Englehart, who went mad with grief. She had a beautiful little boy and a wonderful husband, both of whom died. She had come from a poor family and had felt disrespected much of her childhood. When she and her husband fell in love, her status in the community rose, and with the gorgeous young boy, they were much loved and admired. Well, first the husband and then the boy took sick and passed. When the boy died, she refused to accept it. She carried the dead body from house to house asking for medicine. Our neighbors didn't know what to say or how to help. Liza refused to believe that the small blond boy was gone. She finally came to Grandfather. His reaction shocked me. When she approached him, her eyes were insane with sorrow.

"Do you have any medicine for my boy?" she asked.

He answered, "Yes. I think I can help."

I stood behind him, speechless.

"Leave the boy with me," he said. "I know a medicine that no one else knows."

Liza's face momentarily relaxed.

"What we need is mustard seeds," he told her.

"I have them," she announced quickly.

"Not just any mustard seeds," he said. "I need you to go into Pelynt and knock on every door, and, with all the humility you can find, tell them you are looking for the home where no one has died. And when you find it . . . ask them for their mustard seeds. Then bring them immediately to me. I will watch your boy until you return."

Poor, sweet Liza was delighted. "I will return," she vowed.

Well, you can imagine, every home she went to, she heard stories from bereaved men and women who could offer no mustard seeds. Sadly, family after family told her tales of the loved ones they had lost. When she returned to our door, she looked a thousand years old but clearly had regained her mind. Grandfather and she held a small cremation ceremony on the hill behind our stables. I helped light the fire.

He held her hand. "Obviously, everything must pass. But have faith that wherever your boy has gone, we will soon go too. Whatever is happening is happening to all of us."

I know I should go to sleep now, but there is an owl outside my window who calls out for me to continue writing to you. Somehow I feel that, as long as I keep pen to paper, we will still be close.

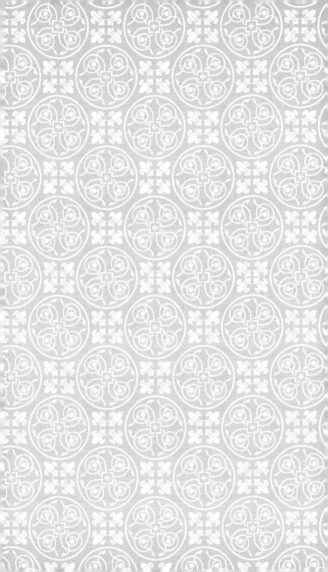

XVIII

Equality

EVERY knight holds human equality as an unwavering truth. A knight is never present when men or women are being degraded or compromised in any way, because if a knight were present, those committing the hurtful acts or words would be made to stop.

Mary-Rose, Cven, and Idamay, here you can see into Grandfather's position on equality between the genders. Certainly there are many differences of experience when we are walking through this life as either a man or a woman, but the essential truths are the same for both. Many of history's greatest knights have in fact been women, though too often small-minded rulers have called these women by less flattering names.

When I think of equality, I can almost hear the opening phrases of "The Ballad of the Forty-Four-Pointed Red Deer." I know your mother loves to sing this song to you children, but you may not know that I taught her the lyrics.

The first time I heard the song, it was late one evening, two days' ride north from London, where the Knights of Lanhydrock made camp. It was strange country to me, moody and moving with a ghostlike breeze. We'd had an extremely fine day hunting. I had with me my first hawk. Grandfather had sent all the way to Norway for it. Its eyes had been sewn shut since birth (I know you hate this, Mary-Rose!) and it was as tame and obedient as our best hounds. This hawk had found for us the largest red deer I have ever seen; it was a thirty-two-pointed stag weighing more than four men could carry.

We made camp inside a ring of large stones. The rocks had been arranged by an ancient, forgotten people and seemed to hold a hidden power. Some of the more superstitious of our men were scared to sleep inside the ring, but Grandfather and I were drawn to its mysterious power. We made a fire in the center, and soon all the men were camped around us. The oldest among us, Sir Angus Doyle, was the only one to pitch his tent outside the circle.

"You've grown silly in your years, old man," Grandfather called out to Sir Doyle.

"I'm not scared of the rocks," the grizzled, gray knight said. "I just don't want to be near the fools who killed that beautiful stag."

"He was beautiful," I said. "I think we were all sad to see him fall."

"But fools we are not," Sir Richard shouted out, patting his big potbelly. "This is the finest meal we have had in years!"

"Young knights"—Doyle scowled towards Grandfather—"they talk of chivalry, they talk of honor and equality, and yet you kill a thirty-two-pointed red deer in the center of the old forest. You don't even know 'The Ballad,' do you?"

We looked at one another, unsure of what Old Doyle was referring to.

"They do not," Grandfather said quietly.

"Even I remember barely a fragment. Please come by the fire and sing for us. Don't be angry. Teach us."

The old master knight stepped out of the darkness and sat with his back to one of the great stones, his face lit by the dancing light of the fire.

"A long time ago, these great stones all around us held a roof. And on that roof was a statue of a forty-four-pointed red deer" (Idamay, forty-four points means he had forty-four tips to his antlers).

Old Doyle then sang "The Ballad of the Forty-Four-Pointed Red Deer." The melody is piercing, as you know, but Old Doyle didn't sing it like your mother does.

His voice was creaky and broken, as if the song were being sung by the swaying trees above us. You kids know this song well, but understand this was the first time I'd heard it. Imagine hearing those lyrics sung at night, near the very circle of stones the ballad speaks of, by the oldest man left alive. Spiders ran through the bones of my back. Ghosts from the last thousand years swam in the air around us.

The little child said, Please, Mother, please tell
Of the great Red Stag who said, all shall be
*   well.*
The Red Deer King, a hart of forty-four,
Who put an end to Edvard's terrible war.

This story is old, as ancient as time,
A fable from the earth told in rhyme.
Like phases of the moon, or the sun's rise,
The pull of the ocean, it's constant and wise.

As the old knight Doyle finished the ballad and we all listened to the final chorus of the story of that magnificent deer who sacrificed himself for the other animals of the forest, each of us looked around at the dancing shadows of the great stones. I imagined what the roof must have looked like long ago and wished I could have seen the statue of the great animal. Some of our men, I gathered, were less hypnotized and started grumbling. "That was long! What was the point of that old song, Doyle?"

"It was a pretty melody," Sir Richard offered. "But really, Doyle, you know deer can't talk!" Everyone laughed.

"Sir Doyle is saying," Grandfather scolded, "that often people who claim to be knights are among the smug and self-righteous. Convinced we understand everything that's happening around us, we consider ourselves among the fair, noble, and wise, or even believe that we are doing all we can. When it is obvious, most of us don't think very deeply at all, and each one of us has far to aspire before we can claim we have even really done our best."

I made it a point to learn the song.

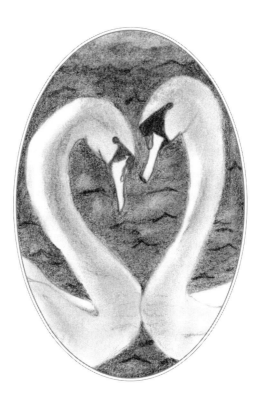

XIX

Love

LOVE is the end goal. It is the music of our lives. There is no obstacle that enough love cannot move.

The magnificent knights and ladies of this world have been great leaders and warriors, but also healers. They fight with love, lead with love, and heal with love.

This does not mean they skirt or evade confrontation. Sometimes you must fight for your beliefs. Confrontation is always preferable to dishonesty, or injustice. A knight is never goaded into battle but enters the fray with a lucid mind, free from fear, anger, or vengeance. In this way he can be sure that the options of peaceful resolution have been exhausted, as well as better position himself for victory.

If you are unable to control your anger, keep your distance and your mouth shut until you can. It is easy to intimidate or to make others feel small or afraid; this is not strength. A great knight or lady uses power to empower others. Do the good you have the power to do.

Protect the young, watch your siblings' backs, and care for the elderly; you will find no better use of your time. Be careful not to draw the circle of your family too small. There is no finite amount of love.

In courtship, honesty is the first requisite. To achieve honesty, a knight must first be intimate with his own soul. This is difficult and takes time. Just as we all have secret thoughts and concerns inside ourselves, which we would share only with a person we value, respect, and trust, so too is it with the body. There are secret places that we need not share, which need not to be shared.

A knight is never in a hurry. He is careful with his heart and the hearts of others. Beware of feigning affection; it is never necessary. You show others the most respect by being truthful, not by trying to please them. Know that "love" is more than a word; it is an action.

Do not make the common mistake of confusing love with desire or obsession. Be suspicious of too much passion. It can turn love into a kind of malady that is as destructive as too much wine. To love is to bring well-being to the object of our affection. Love is responsible, safe; it has care in it.

I met your mother when she was sixteen. It's a long, embarrassing story for me, but you deserve to know. When your mother and I first met, I was in love with the Duchess of York, along with everyone else. I'd met the duchess only once, but no sooner did we make eye contact than I was madly, deeply, irrevocably "in love." I had dreams every night that she would be my bride. She looked ravishing in her elaborate gowns, jeweled from head to toe, with a handmaiden at each side. Oh! I yearned for her to notice me. We would be the most famous couple in the world! I imagined.

Well, it didn't turn out so well. I sent her a long love letter designed to show her that not only was I the bravest knight in all the land but I was a great poet too! It seemed to work, at first. I was invited to a series of dances and became one of the duchess's thirty or so suitors. Several times I was granted a walk in the garden, and twice I was even invited for a cup of tea. Slowly, I began to suspect that I was merely a pawn in a game designed to win Prince Philip's favor. One day, her secretary wrote me asking that I please not write or visit again. I was despondent. Her marriage to the Prince was announced officially a week later. But I refused to accept defeat. I was bent on one thing: winning back her love and stopping this sham of a royal wedding. Obviously, the duchess should be with me!

Then there was an unexpected turn of events. Quite suddenly, one quarter of our house burnt down. We still don't know exactly how it happened; our fireplace was old and in disrepair, and I think in my depression it may have been my fault. I may have left some unused kindling too close to the fire. The house was severely damaged, and even worse, Grandfather was injured. In trying to put out the fire, he had suffered severe burns and was in terrible pain. He did not blame me, he was angry he hadn't repaired the chimney, but I couldn't shake a feeling of guilt and culpability. There was a woman who lived twenty miles away who was said to be skilled in healing burns. When I called on her, I discovered the woman had recently died. Her daughter, however, said she could help. This was my first introduction to your mother.

With her riding on the back of my horse the entire twenty-mile journey home, I confessed to your mother my terrible feelings of guilt that the fire might have been my fault. I'm ashamed to say, I also mentioned to her the terribly important tale of my passion and unreciprocated true love for the Duchess of York. We talked and talked. Twice a week we made this journey, there and back. Your mother was a wonderful nurse, quickly eased Grandfather's pain, and hastened his healing. Patiently she listened and advised me in my follies with the duchess and helped me to forgive myself for the accident. Grandfather would survive, and I would have ample opportunity to be of service to him.

When Grandfather no longer needed treatment, I found myself writing to your mother daily. At first I just wrote reports of Grandfather's progress, but later our letters became more personal. Over a period of several years we became good friends. Your mother is a wonderful writer and reveals her true nature in her small, clear handwriting and her succinct observations. She made me laugh. Oddly enough, I'd never even considered her romantically. I was too concerned with my duties, and my general disappointments with myself. By the time your mother and I first danced at her cousin Philpa's wedding, I realized like a slap to the face that I loved this woman, body and soul, and had for quite some time. How strange that I never even saw it coming. The whole of my boyhood I had expected love to be wild, grand, all-encompassing, and over-whelming. With your mother it had felt too healthy, honest, and wholesome to be love. After we danced, when everyone was tumbling outdoors, we accidentally kissed. It was awkward, and neither one of us was sure how it had happened or what would happen next. Later that evening I watched her play the dulcimer. Her intellect, her body, and her emotions seemed to be absolutely one. Her chest rose and fell as she played. She wasn't merely breathing; it was more as if she were being breathed. From that moment forward she held my beating heart in the palms of her hands.

I didn't "fall in love" with your mother at first sight the way I had heard about it in song, or as I had experienced with the duchess. No, it happened slowly, and because of that, I could never "fall out of love." There was no "falling" at all. It has been a subtle, ever-growing relationship. One that has given me energy, joy, moments of pure bliss, laughter, romance—but more than anything we have been and always will be friends. I know that's probably not the fairy tale young people want to hear. But I promise, if I were allowed one wish, it would be for each of you to feel the kind of love I feel for, and from, your mother.

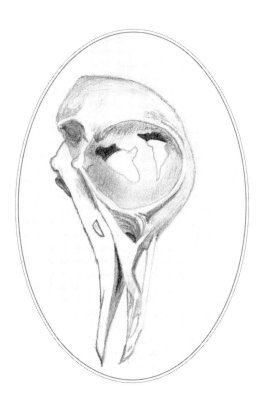

XX

Death

LIFE is a long series of farewells; only the circumstances should surprise us. A knight concerns himself with gratitude for the life he has been given. He does not fear death, for the work one knight begins, others may finish.

How a knight lives is what is important, not on which particular afternoon he was born or on which specific morning he might die. That is why I do not want you to mourn inappropriately for me. Regardless of the outcome of today's struggle, I will continue. The past and future are alive in each passing instant. Eternity is not something that begins at the moment of death, it is happening now.

Late in his life, Grandfather became very ill and knew he did not have long to live. Despite the teachings of his elders and the wisdom he had attained, he suddenly became terribly afraid to die. He had accomplished much in his eight decades of life but longed to do more.

He felt defeated, his body ached, and he was unable to do many of the things he loved—things he had assumed he would always do, until that day when death would suddenly take him away. But death did not come suddenly; it was coming slowly, and he knew it. He was a shadow of the man I had known. He thought, if only he had done things differently he would not have grown weak.

Grandfather was not perfect. At his best, he was the most remarkable human I have ever known, but some of those last days were not his finest. His body was in so much pain that he could not listen to anyone, not Grandmother, and certainly not me.

One afternoon he slipped away from us, put on his finest armor, went out to the stable, and saddled his old horse, Triumph. They rode off towards the ocean. I was going to follow him and make sure he didn't fall, but Grandmother told me to let him alone. "If he wants to stir up death," she said, "let him."

When he came upon the sandy cliffs where our land meets the sea, he sat on top of his stallion, staring at the waves crashing one after another, hour after hour until it was dark. And still he sat there. He stared off into the black horizon, periodically falling asleep upon his tired horse.

Eventually the light dawned again and morning arrived. Underneath his legs he could feel Triumph begin to twitch with exhaustion and hunger. Triumph was old too. Grandfather dismounted and said good-bye to his trusted friend. They had won many victories together, but the old knight was beginning to realize that this battle must be fought alone. Still, he could not help but be surprised when the horse finally wandered off. He felt abandoned by his friend, and his loneliness seemed intolerable. He sat down on the beach, his meticulously polished steel armor now dusted with salt and sand.

All his life he had lived by the Rules, and they had supported him. He had always tried to think of himself like a tree with an extensive root system, gaining nourishment from many elements: his wife, his children, his friends, his work, his service, his community. Why did he feel so lonely now? Why did his accomplishments seem so empty? Why did his former ambitions feel so vain? He had been blessed with a long, healthy life, and for the most part he had handled it wisely. Not always, but almost always he remembered to want what he had and not to covet the things he did not have. But what about his coming death, when he would have absolutely nothing? Nothing at all. When he himself would not even exist? Oh no! He was terribly afraid. He did not want to die. He loved his wife. She was good to him and he to her. Every morning when he awoke he would thank her for choosing him. He knew that there were many fine men in the world, and sometimes his eyes would tear in gratitude that she had picked him to share her life with, and she felt the same about him. Why could she not come with him? Eventually she would join him, he reassured himself, but his faith felt hollow. Still, the waves crashed again and again. He felt so terribly adrift. Not since he was a boy had he felt this lost. Had he done something wrong? Had he not loved his neighbors? Had he failed the knight's code? Why was it not supporting him now? In anger he took off his armor and threw it piece by piece into the sea. Exposed and vulnerable, he thought, What is so important about me, this person who happens to be named Lemuel Green of Pynzant? Stillness settled over him. He looked again at the waves, as they tossed his armor about along the shore. Slowly he remembered that he was not the only one dying. There were many dying at each and every instant, and many being born. He was not alone. He could hear, mixed in with the sound of the waves, the infants taking their first breaths, the mothers crying with pain and joy, the last stifled gasps of the dying. He could hear the sound of his whole generation being carried out to sea like the waves crashing against the shore and then swishing back again. When one wave was gone, nothing had been lost, and nothing had been gained. The waves had always been, and still were, simply water. The ocean remained unaltered. For a moment, he was not afraid. A familiar, great, and holy silence seemed to rise around him. He could not and did not conquer death, but one thing he had learned in his long life was that if he understood something, things were just as they were, and if he did not understand something, things were still simply just as they were. Having an understanding, however, gave him less fear and more confidence. He smiled to himself—what had he been so scared of? He had died so many times already. The boy who was an arrow retriever at the Battle of Agincourt had been gone for a long time. The young man who married his wife? Gone. The grown man who led the Knights of Lanhydrock into so many battles? Gone. This old man would soon be gone too. Slowly he began to whistle. He whistled like a bird standing on a fragile branch, who sings even though he knows that soon the bending bough will break. He sings because he knows he has wings. Grandfather threw his sword into the ocean and walked home. Triumph was happy to see him again. Grandmother scolded him for being gone so long, and without even a proper coat. I remember we were all upset with him for causing so much alarm. That evening, sitting by the fire, Grandfather recounted the story to me. Calmer now, he seemed much more himself.

Grandmother walked back into the room and asked, "Well, do you want to eat or go to sleep?"

I answered that I thought he should have a little something warm to eat.

As she left the room, Grandfather whispered, "You must be much more intelligent than I am."

"Why's that?" I laughed.

"Because whenever anybody asks you a question," he grumbled through the large gap in his front teeth, "you always have an answer at the ready. As for me, I have to think before I speak."

We both sat silently looking at the fire.

That night, as your mother was helping prepare the food and I was putting you, Lemuel, to bed, Grandfather fell asleep and died. I imagine his armor and sword still sit at the bottom of the sea, covered by oysters, with schools of minnows swimming through his crumbling chest plate. He, however, is gone.

It is morning now. Cold air bites at my fingers and beckons me back to the warmth of our home. How I wish this moment had not arrived. Someday, someone else will explain to you the unacceptable situation our people have been forced into, but for now, be assured that I have no misgivings about our knights or the cause at hand. I only wish my responsibilities to our collective good did not stand so directly at odds with my responsibility to you.

Please forgive the length of this letter. The owl that was keeping me company has long flown away. I look back and count these pages and see I have been most self-indulgent. These are all lessons you will learn on your own. The sun has come up, and foolishly I have not slept for a moment. As you can tell, I have much left to learn.

One last thought. (Please forgive me! But if I stop writing I worry it really will be good-bye!) There is a memory that won't let me go. Last summer all you children were playing by the ocean. We were with your mother and her sister's family, do you remember? The weather was sublime, streaks of sun and a deep blue sky. You four and all your cousins were building castles with the warm, muddy sand. Each of you kept your castle separate, announcing, "This one is mine!" "That's yours!" "Stay away from mine!"

When all the castles were finished, your cousin Wallace playfully stepped on Cven's. Lemuel, you flew into a protective rage. You were only looking out for your sister, I know. Mary-Rose, you thought Lemuel was overreacting, and you threw him to the ground. Next, everyone was fighting, throwing sand, howling with tears, and pushing one another. Young Wally had to be taken home, sobbing in your aunt's arms. When he was gone, you all went back to playing with your castles for a little while but quickly moved on to swimming. It grew cloudy, and soon it was time for us to begin the journey home. No one cared at all about their castle anymore. Idamay, you stamped on yours. Cven, you toppled yours with both hands. We all went home. And the gentle rain washed all the castles back into the surf.

Please be kind to one another.

I love all of you and know you older children wish you could ride with me today, but I am grateful beyond what you can imagine that you are all safe at home. If we do not meet again in this life, know that, as each new year passes, I will be in the autumn wind that rustles the leaves at your feet, the winter snowflakes that freeze your cheeks, the rains of spring that drench your hair, and the hot summer sun that burns your arms. I will be with you always.

Remember me.

Your loving father,
Thomas

The Ballad of the Forty-Four-Pointed Red Deer

The little child said, "Please, Mother, please
   tell
Of the great Red Stag who said, all shall be
   well.
The Red Deer King, a hart of forty-four,
Who put an end to Edvard's terrible war."

This story is old, as ancient as time,
A fable from the earth told in rhyme.
Like phases of the moon, or the sun's rise,
The pull of the ocean, it's constant and wise.

One spring morning, when Stonehenge was
   new,

A doe and her fawn tripped wet through the
   dew.
Undaunted and curious, "Mother," said the
   fawn,
"Of whom is that statue in the center of the
   lawn?"

"My sweet one," said she, "that magnificent
   stone
Erected by Edvard the Elder, to stand alone,
'Tis the likeness, my son, of our own Stag
   King,
Who the day you were born did a marvelous
   thing!"

"The day I was born? Oh, tell me the story!
How is my birthday the day of his glory?"
"That's why I brought you inside here, my son,
To tell you the tale of all that was done.

"A tale of two mighty kings.
A tale of woeful and wondrous things.
On that day I carried my child inside,
The day when my child and I nearly died.

"On this very spot the story takes place.
This is the grass where I first saw his face.
The warrior King who struck all with dread,
Hunting us down, wanting us dead."

"What was the reason? Why did he kill?"
"Why did he hunt us? Why? For the thrill.
He loved the game. He loved the chase.
The smell of our fear made his cruel heart
    race.

"He'd feast on our bodies, our muscles, our
    meat;
Our tongues and our eyes he thought
    deliciously sweet."
The young deer stuttered and stammered,
    "Oh, no!"
"'Tis true," said his mother. "This Edvard
    did so.

"So listen, so listen
To this marvelous story
Of my dear child's birth
And the Stag King's glory!

153

" 'Twas the hunt Edvard loved, the hunt that
    was all.
His scabbard gold, the sword eager to fall.
His bow and blade never left his arm,
Prayer bored him, worse was the farm.

"His once healthy country had now become
    idle.
His sleek white stallion was ever in bridle.
Shopkeepers and tailors were forced from
    their fronts,
The carpenters and farmers were made to
    join hunts.

"Tools were left dropped in the silt.
Barns unfinished, homes half built.
Potters left clay, and cobblers their shoes.
Schoolhouses were empty, for poets, no muse.

"The people wanted more than a bow and a
    knife.
The people had blood, but they wanted a life!
Matters, they took into their own hands,
Fencing the deer into one large stand.

154

"This way when Edvard wanted his meat,
The killing would be easy, a corral for his
    treats.
When the King saw the fences around the
    deer,
He stared at the creatures, soft and sincere.

"'So my people don't want to hunt you beasts,
They would rather to other pursuits be
    released.
And a king must abide by his subjects' eyes.'
Edvard the Elder thought himself wise.

"Two stags, one white with points a full score,
One more glorious, red with points forty-four.
'Those two,' said Edvard, 'those two must
    live.
Do not hunt them. To them, their lives,
    I give.'"

"Mother," said the fawn, cherishing the word,
"Wasn't the red deer king of both herds?"
"He is our king now, Son. Be patient. Be bold.
Listen to the story. All will be told.

"The people left safe, went back to their
   homes.
The deer, from the fence, were no longer to
   roam.
Shooting one deer a day, meat was easy to
   gain.
'Now, all is simple' was the hunter's refrain.

"Not so, however, for the trapped forest deer.
Many were pierced by the arrows so near.
Not just the unfortunate with the arrow in his
   side.
'Twere many trampled, as they tried to hide.

"One killed, but many more maimed.
Every day the terror was the same.
Hunters in the morning, fear would ignite.
Deer scrambled to escape the fight.

"Approaching the White Stag of our herd,
The Red Hart, with him, exchanged a word.
Offering one of their own, every other day,
The madness and confusion might be driven
   away.

"A terrible solution, but suffering would be
  eased.
Heads solemn, the stags were far from pleased.
To each herd the terrible situation was
  explained.
A buck drew the lot, from his face the blood
  drained.

"When the hunters saw the buck trembling
  alone,
'Remarkable deer!' they said. 'Wisdom
  they've shown.'
An arrow flew, piercing the buck's heart.
This was the day the tradition did start.

"Mornings a deer to doom was sent.
On and on, for weeks it went.
Till the lot fell to one exceptionally mild,
A doe whose belly was swollen with child.

"'Twas I, and the child I carried 'twas you.
My mind was cloven. What would I do?
The terms of the lottery were crystal clear.
We would die. My pulse drummed with fear.

"'I beg you,' I said, on all four knees.
'White King, the lot has fallen to me.
Inside my womb there's a child to be born.
Willingly, I will leave my fawn forlorn.

"'Once he's able to live on his own,
I will pay the price with skin and bone.
I will go, but spare my child, please.'
'No,' said the Stag, 'your pain cannot ease.

"'The lottery has fallen. You must die.'
'Oh!' I wailed, tears in my eye.
Crestfallen, desperate, on the ocean tossed,
My life and yours both would be lost.

"Blessed, the Stag of Forty-Four was near.
Hearing my troubles, he said, 'Sweet deer,
Till your fawn is born, LIVE! GO!
Fly and be at peace. All is not woe.'

"Grateful beyond words, I bounded away.
Eluding death till another dark day.
But one question yet that I still had to face.

The fact that another would be forced in my
   place.

"In the forest, evenly falls the rain.
Someone else would feel my pain.
The Red Hart walked towards the arrows.
Saying good-bye, he glanced at the sparrows.

"Ask another to make the sacrifice?
Not the Red Hart. He would pay my price.
From a distance, I watched the coming assault.
Only now I understood, this was all my fault.

"The hunters looked down on the great being.
They couldn't believe what they were seeing.
Edvard arrived with his men and his flag.
'Look, Sire, it's the forty-four-pointed stag!'

" 'What are you doing, you beautiful beast?
You were not made for my royal feast!
I spared you and the White Stag from the
   game.
Strong are you; send me the lame.'

"'I have come,' said the Hart, 'to take the place
of a doe with child. Her fate I will face.
Two should not die, so here I have come,
Bury my bones when you are done.'

"From a slumber the King was now awake,
From this hart a lesson he could take.
'Lay down your life so another will not fall?'
Edvard stared at the antlers held tall.

"'I will,' the Stag replied, 'and I shall.
I am not afraid, all shall be well.
Death is a small price for the gift of life.
What if the doe had been my wife?'

"Tugging at his whiskers, staring at the deer,
Edvard said, 'I am glad you're here.
Care for the least, is what a king must do.
So in payment for a teaching so true,

"'You and your herd may go free.
Teach the others as you've taught me.
Take your kin. Live in peace.
All are spared. Your family released.'

"The strong Stag shook his heavy head.
'O King of men, this wood is my bed,
If I leave with my herd, if we turn to go,
The remaining will suffer, this we know.

" 'Day and night your arrows shall fall.
For years in anguish my friends will call.
What would be gained at such a cost?
The doe and fawn I saved would be lost.'

" 'But these other deer are none of your own.'
The Hart resolutely stood on a stone.
Again Edvard tugged and pulled at his beard.
'Stag, you inspire.' His throat he cleared.

" 'I see the garden of your mind's been
    unweeded,
This is a great lesson,' the King conceded.
'From this stockade of death all will be freed.'
'King,' answered the Hart, 'you are noble
    indeed.'

"Edvard responded, 'Go, live in peace.'
The Stag again refused to be released.

A stillness settled, a rabbit stopped and stared.
No one could believe what the great Hart dared.

"So listen, so listen
To this marvelous story
Of my dear child's birth
And the Stag King's glory!

"The forest was watching, twisted in fret.
'Too long have I lived with danger to let
It fall so heavily on my friends now.
Sufferings elsewhere though I know not how.

"'The madness of murder, chaos, fear.
Too long I have held these feelings near.
If we walk away, what creatures are next?
There's no honor under this pretext.

"'Without limit or mercy, now all will be
    killed.
With blood and bones the soil will be tilled.
Abandon the forest and be at peace with
    myself?
Knowing that others pay for my wealth.

" 'If you can free us all, merciful King,
Legend awaits, freedom will ring.
If you really intend to be at peace,
Not only the deer must be released.'

"Edvard could not believe what he was hearing.
The eyes of his men behind him were leering.
Again he sighed. His head began to fall.
'You will make crop farmers of us all!

" 'You are a teacher and I your student.
All will be free. It is most prudent.
There, I am finished. It will be done.
The game is played. You have won.

" 'My men and I must practice what we
    preach.
We understand the cost of the wisdom you
    teach.
The woods will be wild, free and singing.
You have struck the bell and it is ringing.

" 'Run in the fields, enjoy the sun,
Live long and know what you have done

For all the wild forest beasts,
From the greatest to the least.'

"Deep in the woodland the sparrows sang
     a song.
But the great Stag did not trot along.
Gently he shook his antlers side to side
And looked out as an eagle did glide.

"The swallows danced, he saw them play.
In the trees a falcon, an owl, a jay.
'See the brightly feathered fliers
That sing so sweetly, the Lord's true friars.

"'Alas, Your Majesty,' the Stag quietly
     said,
'Soon now they will all be dead.
Can you, King, tell me why?
Your slings will crash upon the sky,

"'With a wrath they have never known.
Repeat the kindness you have shown.
Open your heart not just halfway,
Free the birds this September day!'

" 'Good Heavens! And I thought I was strong!'
The warrior bit his lip. 'But you are wrong.
You are pious, unrelenting, and stubborn.'
The Hart stood undaunted and offered in
    turn,

" 'To lead, we exchange the paved road for
    rougher.
Can we be happy, if others suffer?
The straight road does not bend.
No peace unless to all it extends.'

"The tall King slipped off his proud horse,
His powerful hand on his sword, of course.
Right up to the great Stag he stalked,
He spit on the ground before he talked.

" 'And what of the fishes?' Edvard hissed.
'The rainbow trout, will he not be missed?'
The King and the Hart stood eye to eye.
'For their freedom will you not want to try?'

" 'You are wise, great King, to consider the
    lakes,

Ponds, and streams. Thought must we take.
Were we to abandon those silver swimmers,
Who bring life to all the shimmering rivers,

" 'The fate of the ocean might be death,
Then we would not enjoy a breath.
It would weigh so heavily on our head
We'd wish it were we that were dead.

" 'If we do not speak for these silent ones,
For the salmon who upstream so brilliantly
    run,
For catfish in the dark, who do we think will?'
The Stag's eyes penetrated, the King felt the
    thrill.

" 'Are vegetables tasty when eaten alone?
Are grains? Fruit? What of a scone?
This now seems to be my only source,
For nourishment I'll have no other recourse.

" 'You drive a hard bargain, now I am in
    terror,
Yet I see in your thought no visible error.

Your logic stands tall as an old oak tree.
For any to have peace, even the fish must be
    free.'

"Edvard the Elder called to his attendants.
'Throughout my realm I will make an
    amendment.
From this day, liberated are all living beings.
With my heart now open, my eyes are seeing.

"'To all beings that fear harm as me
This is my true wish and lasting decree.
None shall be hunted, none trapped, nor
    killed.
To all my children this I have willed.'

"Edvard turned back to the powerful Hart.
'Stag, I hope you see this as a start.
Content? Can you now breathe in peace?
Now that the rest of the forest is unleashed.'

"The Hart looked around at the woods with
    joy,
The birds all flying, as if the sky were a toy.

The squirrels, the foxes, even the ducks
Were giggling and laughing at their good luck.

"A tear fell from the strong Hart's eye.
'Yes,' he said with a herculean sigh,
A single tear that reflected the earth.
Everyone was shown what they're worth.

"Forty-four sparrows landed on his great rack,
Singing this melody with no fear of attack.
Then leaping away like a young fawn,
He bounded across this very lawn.

"'Open the gates,' Edvard's voice did resound.
The fences were playfully knocked to the
      ground.
Deer scattered, running light as a feather.
Edvard's heart was warm as the weather.

"And then Edvard the Elder built as he should
This circle of stones with a roof so all could
Rejoice, remember, sing, and hear
'The Ballad of the Forty-Four-Pointed Red
      Deer.'"

"It's true?" whispered the fawn. "You and I
    were here?"
He spoke so soft she could barely hear,
The lad's legs bouncing, unable to behave.
"We were the ones the great King saved?"

"Yes, you were born that afternoon
Here on the grass not a moment too soon.
Imagine," said the deer's mother,
"So many being kind to one another."

The little fawn said, "Please, Mother, please
    tell
Of the great Red Stag who said, all shall be
    well.
The Red Deer King, a hart of forty-four,
Who put an end to Edvard's terrible war."

Special Thanks to Other Knights

Muhammad Ali, A. H. Almaas, Marcus Aurelius, Sullivan Ballou, Seymour Bernstein, Sam Creely, the Desert Fathers, "Desiderata," Emily Dickinson, Vincent D'Onofrio, Frederick Douglass, Peter Drucker, Bob Dylan, Dwight D. Eisenhower, Ralph Waldo Emerson, Laurence Fishburne, E. M. Forster, Viktor Frankl, Charles Gaines, Howard L. Green, Leslie Green Hawke, Woody Guthrie, Dag Hammarskjöld, James and Gay Hawke, Ryan Hawke, Robert Hughes, Victor Hugo, Catherine Ingram, Eli Keefe Jackson, Julian of Norwich, John Keats, Martin Luther King Jr., Lao Tzu, Mother Ann Lee, C. S. Lewis, Richard Linklater, Vince Lombardi, George Lucas, Nelson Mandela, Rafe Martin, Thomas Merton, Thich Nhat Hanh, Andrew Niccol, Anaïs Nin, Eugene O'Neill, Joseph Papp, Saint Paul, River Phoenix, Heather Powers, Patrick Powers Jr. and Sr., Branch Rickey, Paul Robeson, Carl Rogers, Eleanor Roosevelt, William Shakespeare, Jonathan Marc Sherman, Sir Tom Stoppard, Mother Teresa, J.R.R. Tolkien, Amanda Priest Vandeveer, Kurt Vonnegut Jr., Jennifer Rudolph Walsh, Simone Weil, Jessamyn West, Walt Whitman, Tennessee Williams, and, of course, King Arthur.

All Shall Be Well

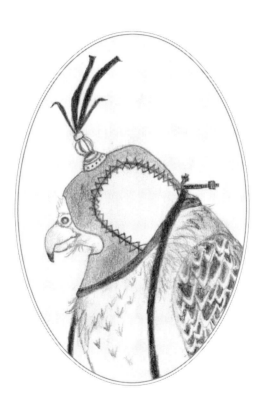

List of Rules

I. Solitude (honey buzzard feather)

II. Humility (winter wren)

III. Gratitude (black-winged stilt)

IV. Pride (rooster)

V. Cooperation (bean geese)

VI. Friendship (long-tailed tits)

VII. Forgiveness (mallard duckling)

VIII. Honesty (little owl)

IX. Courage (kestrel)

X. Grace (sedge warbler)

XI. Patience (robin's eggs in nest)

XII. Justice (sparrow hawk)

XIII. Generosity (common spoonbill)

XIV. Discipline (grey heron)

XV. Dedication (great spotted woodpecker)

XVI. Speech (bluethroat)

XVII. Faith (barn swallow)

XVIII. Equality (tawny owl)

XIX. Love (mute swans)

XX. Death (blackbird skull)

A NOTE ABOUT THE AUTHOR

A four-time Academy Award nominee, twice for writing and twice for acting, Ethan Hawke has starred in the films *Dead Poets Society, Reality Bites, Gattaca,* and *Training Day* as well as Richard Linklater's *Before Sunrise* trilogy and *Boyhood.* He is the author of the novels *The Hottest State* and *Ash Wednesday.* He lives in Brooklyn with his four children and this book's illustrator, Ryan Hawke.

A NOTE ON THE TYPE

This book was set in a version of Monotype Baskerville, the antecedent of which was a typeface designed by John Baskerville (1706–1775). Baskerville, a writing master in Birmingham, England, began experimenting around 1750 with type design and punch cutting. His first book, published in 1757 and set throughout in his new types, was a Virgil in royal quarto. It was followed by other famous editions from his press. Baskerville's types, which are distinctive and elegant in design, were a forerunner of what we know today as the "modern" group of typefaces.

Composed by North Market Street Graphics,
Lancaster, Pennsylvania

Printed and bound by Thomson-Shore,
Dexter, Michigan

Designed by Cassandra J. Pappas

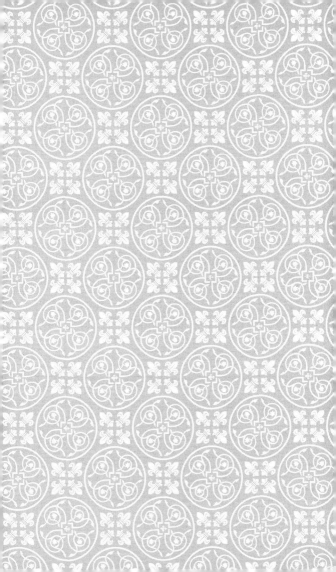

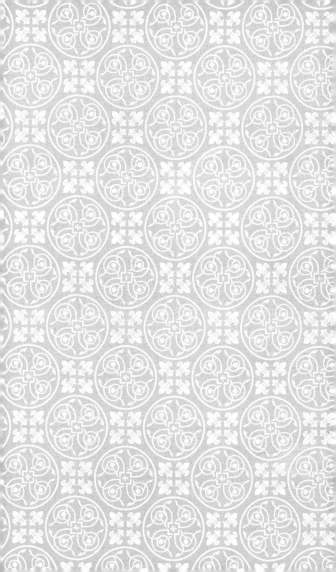